The United Kingdom *Today*

The United Kingdom *Today*

Michael Gallagher

SEA-TO-SEA

Mankato Collingwood London

Designer Peter Bailey/Proof Books
Editor Constance Novis
Art Director Jonathan Hair
Editor-in-Chief John C. Miles
Picture research Sarah Smithies

This edition first published in 2009 by
Sea-to-Sea Publications
Distributed by Black Rabbit Books
P.O. Box 3263
Mankato, Minnesota 56002

Library of Congress Cataloging-in-Publication Data:

Gallagher, Michael.
  The United Kingdom today / Michael Gallagher.
    p. cm. -- (Today)
  Includes index.
  Summary: "Describes the history, geography, and cultures of the United Kingdom,
including cultural differences between its member nations"--Provided by publisher.
  ISBN 978-1-59771-125-8
  1. Great Britain--Juvenile literature. 2. Northern Ireland--Juvenile literature. I. Title.
  DA27.5.G35 2009
  941--dc22
                                2008004575

9 8 7 6 5 4 3 2

Published by arrangement with the Watts Publishing Group Ltd, London.

Picture credits

Inside: Andrew Milligan, Reuters, Corbis: 12. Benedict Luxmoore, Arcaid, Alamy: 31.
British Library, The Art Archive: 6. Chris Barry, Rex Features: 37.
Dagli Orti, A, Fine Art Museum Bilbao, The Art Archive: 16. David Noton Photography, Alamy: 21 (t).
David Poole, Alamy: 18 (b). David Robertson, Alamy: 21(c). Derek Croucher, Corbis: 20.
Gary Merrin , Rex Features: 32. Gianni Muratore , Alamy: 29 (b). GPU, Rex Features: 11.
Greenshoots Communications, Alamy: 40. Hideo Kurihara, Alamy: 22 (l). HL Studios: 46. ICIMAGE, Alamy: 9.
Janine Wiedel Photolibrary, Alamy:19 (b), 36. Jason Smalley, Wildscape, Alamy: 38.
Jayne Fincher, Photo Int, Alamy: 13. JLImages , Alamy: 28-29. John Robertson, Alamy: 26.
Leslie Garland Picture Library, Alamy: 30. Linda Burgess, Alamy: 19 (t). Mary Evans Picture Library, Alamy: 17.
nagelestock.com, Alamy: 24. Peter MacDiarmid, Rex Features: 34. Philippe Hays, Rex Features: 33.
Popperfoto, Alamy: 23 (r). Randy Faris, Corbis: 42. Richard Clune, Corbis: 8. Richard Gardner, Rex Features: 39.
Robin Sanders, Alamy: 27. Sam Morgan Moore, Rex Features: 41. Scott Hortop, Alamy: 18 (c).
Scottish Viewpoint, Alamy: 10. Shout, Rex Features: 43. Sipa Press, Rex Features : 25, 35. Superbild, A1pix: 3, 7.
The Hoberman Collection, Alamy: 15. The Photolibrary Wales, Alamy: 22-23 (c). Visual Arts Library (London), Alamy: 14.

Cover: Front: David Aubrey, Corbis (bc). Jose Fuste Raga, Corbis (br). Richard Clune, Corbis (bl). Superbild, A1pix (t),
Back: Corbis. Superbild, A1pix (b).

Contents

Introduction

Few countries can boast the United Kingdom's wealth of history and tradition. But today, the British are also modernizing fast.

Islands united

Because of the complications of geography, politics, and culture, many people confuse the terms Britain, United Kingdom, and British Isles and, in particular, there is often confusion over exactly what the United Kingdom (or UK) is. To be precise, Great Britain refers only to the island containing three separate countries: England, Scotland, and Wales. It does not include the Northern Ireland, across the Irish Sea. Together though, Great Britain and Northern Ireland make up the state known as the United Kingdom, whose citizens call themselves British. Hundreds of smaller islands such as Anglesey and the Scottish Hebrides also belong to the United Kingdom. The entire group of islands, including Ireland, is known as the British Isles, but this is a geographical term only and does not mean that they are all British possessions.

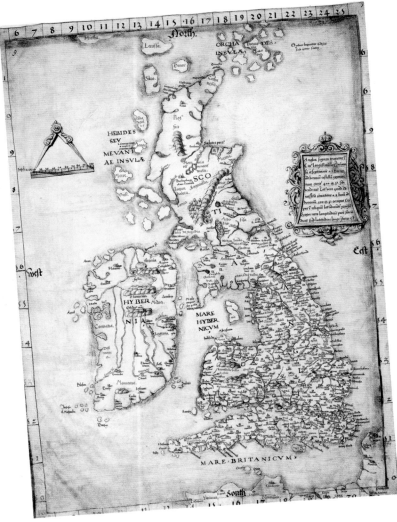

The island of Great Britain—shown in this sixteenth-century map—contains only England, Scotland, and Wales.

"This precious stone set in the silver sea, Which serves it in the office of a wall.... Against the envy of less happier lands."

WILLIAM SHAKESPEARE (1564–1616), PLAYWRIGHT, DESCRIBES ENGLAND

Imperial might

For centuries, the British considered themselves lucky to be islanders, because this helped keep foreign enemies out and enabled seaborne trade to flourish. In fact, by 1850 the UK had become the most powerful state in the world. It had an empire so big the sun never set on all of it, and by the nineteenth century it was the number-one industrial and military power. Today, the UK is no longer as influential, though it has developed a more tolerant and diverse society.

Strength in diversity

The British may have lost their empire, but they have allowed some former colonial subjects to immigrate, and embraced their cultures in the process. Among the native British themselves, a minority of people speak traditional languages such as Scots, Gaelic, and Welsh. And some people even find it difficult to understand the English spoken in numerous regional dialects. However, this variety is reflected in the UK's success in the arts, fashion, and design.

Many traditional industrial areas have fallen on hard times, yet the economy remains one of the world's biggest. Today the southeast of England is one of the richest regions in Europe —with a very high cost of living to match.

The United Kingdom's Union Flag. Technically it can only be called a "Jack" when flown from the jack-staff of a ship.

Symbol of unity: the Union Flag

The United Kingdom's national flag is called the Union Flag but is also known as the Union Jack. It is actually three flags in one, representing the union of England and Wales with Scotland and Northern Ireland. The flag of England (a red cross on a white background) is superimposed on the Scottish saltire (a white diagonal cross on a blue background) and the Irish cross of Saint Patrick (a red diagonal cross on a white background). The Welsh dragon does not appear on the flag, because at the time that the Union Jack was designed, Wales was considered to be part of England.

GEOGRAPHY	Location	Island	POLITICS Status	Nationality of citizens
ENGLAND	British Isles	Great Britain	Part of UK	British
SCOTLAND	British Isles	Great Britain	Part of UK	British
WALES	British Isles	Great Britain	Part of UK	British
N. IRELAND	British Isles	Ireland	Part of UK	British and/or Irish
REPUBLIC OF IRELAND	British Isles	Ireland	Independent republic	Irish
CHANNEL ISLANDS	British Isles	Channel Islands	UK crown dependency	British
ISLE OF MAN	British Isles	Isle of Man	UK crown dependency	British

Geography: Shaped by the seas

Thanks to its location, the UK enjoys a gentle climate and fine scenery, all close to mainland Europe.

Warming effect

The British Isles sit just off the northwestern coast of Europe, between Scandinavia and the Atlantic Ocean. Their northerly location would make for a very cold climate were it not for the curious ocean current known as the Gulf Stream, which brings warmer waters from the Caribbean, helping to raise temperatures and making extreme weather a rarity. Even so, UK weather is notoriously unpredictable. Mild winds from the south can give way to icy blasts from the east, then wet fronts from the Atlantic—sometimes, it seems, all in one day!

The cool, damp climate of the UK produces lush green landscapes such as this one, in Yorkshire.

Subtle beauty

Like the weather, the UK's landscape is not highly dramatic, but it is diverse. There are no mighty rivers or spectacular mountain ranges. Yet it is still a place of great beauty. From the chalky soils of southern England, which rise up in the famous white cliffs at Dover, to the craggy highlands of Scotland, there is huge variety. And because of the climate, much of the land is very fertile. Tiny, picturesque farming villages still exist alongside major cities and smaller market towns. Many British people dream of living in the countryside, although today, the population is overwhelmingly urban.

The Channel Tunnel

In 1994, the British ceased to be an island race, with the opening of their first-ever land link to Europe. Costing $20 billion US to build, the Channel Tunnel is 31 miles (50 km) long and carries trains 131 feet (40 m) below the seabed of the English Channel—one of the world's busiest shipping routes. Passengers can now speed from London to Paris and Brussels in just over two hours, or transport their cars (above) from Great Britain to the French coast in around half an hour.

Uncertain position

Nowhere in the United Kingdom is more than 70 miles (120 km) from the sea, and for centuries, the UK was a great naval power. Nowadays though, most people's experience of maritime life is limited to a trip on one of the many ferries that connect Great Britain to neighboring islands and the rest of Europe.

At its narrowest point, the European mainland is only around 75 miles away from the English coast. But this proximity, combined with the UK's cultural and physical separation, has contributed to an identity crisis among some Britons. Should they forge closer links with their European neighbors, or with English-speaking North America? Or should the UK return to being a completely separate power? It is a question which, so far, the nation has yet to answer.

MAJOR CITIES & POPULATION:

London, England (capital)	7,172,000
Birmingham, England	971,000
Glasgow, Scotland	630,000
Liverpool, England	469,000
Leeds, England	443,000
Edinburgh, Scotland (capital)	430,000
Manchester, England	394,000
Cardiff, Wales (capital)	292,000
Belfast, Northern Ireland (capital)	277,000

FACTFILE : THE UK

Full name: The United Kingdom of Great Britain and Northern Ireland

Location (London): 51°N, 0°W

Total area: 94,500 sq miles (244,755 sq km)

International land borders: 223 miles (360 km) (with Republic of Ireland)

Coastline: 7,723 miles (12,429 km)

Longest river: River Severn (220 miles/354 km)

Highest elevation: 4,406 ft (1,343 km) above sea level (Ben Nevis, Scotland)

Lowest elevation: 13 ft (4 m) below sea level (the Fens, eastern England)

Highest village: 1,525 ft (465 m) above sea level (Flash, Staffordshire)

Average rainfall: 24 in (610 mm)

Average Summer temperature, 2003:
Northern Scotland: 53° F (11.6°C)
SE England: 59.5° F (15.3°C)

Average Winter temperature, 2003:
Northern Scotland: 40° F (4.5°C)
SE England: 43.7° F (6.5°C)

People: Celebrating difference

The British are descended from the many peoples who have settled, invaded, and migrated to their land over the centuries; a process that continues today.

Mixed race

Little is known about the earliest inhabitants of Great Britain. They are thought to have been hunter-gatherers who probably arrived following the northward retreat of ice after the last Ice Age, around 10,000 years ago. Much later though, the Celts, the Romans, the Germanic Angles and Saxons, the Vikings, and lastly, in 1066, the Normans of what is now northern France, invaded Great Britain. Today's native population therefore contains a rich genetic mixture, with ancestral links to some of the native populations of continental Europe.

Celtic fringe

According to popular history, the ancient Britons of the Iron Age were Celts, many of whom were driven westward by Germanic invaders after the Romans left Great Britain around 1,600 years ago. To this day, some British people talk of a western "Celtic fringe" made up of Wales, Scotland, Ireland, and the extreme tip of southwestern England, whose inhabitants believe they differ from the English.

The cultural distinctiveness of the Celtic fringe is most evident in the survival of Gaelic-based languages in Northern Ireland, Wales, Scotland, and the Isle of Man. And, there is still much good-humored rivalry between the "Celts"—especially the fiercely free-spirited Scots— and the English.

Meanwhile, UK society in general is becoming more mixed amid another influx of newcomers.

In parts of Scotland, the Gaelic language is in everyday use. This picture shows a mailman in front of a post office in the Outer Hebrides.

A modern UK city street scene features people of all races and colors, including recent immigrants as well as those whose families have been in the country for generations.

Melting pot

Immigration from the Commonwealth during the twentieth century has brought people of many racial backgrounds to all regions of the UK. The big cities, in particular, have become a magnet for new arrivals, eager to be part of the country's relatively tolerant society. Larger ethnic minorities now include people of Irish, West Indian, southern Asian, and African backgrounds.

In addition, the UK plays its part in offering refuge to those fleeing persecution all over the world. In the last ten years, immigration of all kinds has contributed to one half of the UK's population growth and today, up to 2.6 million inhabitants describe themselves as Muslim, while substantial Jewish, Hindu, and other religious minorities are also thriving. As a whole though, the population is aging, with more than one in six people now over the age of 65. There is a debate over how many immigrants might be needed in future, to replenish the work force.

"A mongrel half-bred race."
— DANIEL DEFOE (1660-1731),
NOVELIST, ON THE ENGLISH

THE UK PEOPLE IN FIGURES
(2004 ESTIMATES)

Population		
	England: 50,093,100	(83.7%)
	Scotland: 5,078,400	(8.5%)
	Wales: 2,952,500	(4.9%)
	Northern Ireland: 1,710,300	(2.9%)
	Total UK: 59,834,300	

Average population growth: 0.4% per year
Average age: 38.6 years
Life expectancy: 75.7 years (male),
80.7 years (female)

Europe's eastern promise

When the European Union admitted ten new member states in 2004 some people feared a very large influx of immigrants into the UK, legally entitled to settle and search for work. In fact, arrivals from former communist states such as Poland and the Czech Republic have been fewer than expected, with around 123,000 people granted work permits in the first year of EU expansion. Many have brought much-needed skills in areas such as medicine and construction.

Politics: A people empowered

The queen is the head of state of the United Kingdom. Real authority, however, lies in the hands of politicians—and not all of them are based in London.

Royalty restrained

The United Kingdom is a constitutional monarchy, which means power is shared between a hereditary monarch and an elected government. Both must observe a supreme body of law called a constitution.

The government is led by a prime minister and a so-called cabinet of ministers who between them are responsible for major issues like health, defense, and foreign policy. It rules in the name of the monarch, currently Queen Elizabeth II, and her influence is restricted to offering consultations, warnings, and advice. However, ministers may be foolish to ignore these, because the queen has now reigned for over half a century. This makes her much more experienced than any elected politician.

A view of the Scottish parliament. In recent years government has moved away—"devolved"—from Westminster.

Parliament supreme

The government must also answer to parliament, which sits in two chambers. Members of the lower chamber, the House of Commons, are elected. The upper chamber, the House of Lords, was traditionally made up of hereditary peers. Today, most of its members are appointed in the name of the queen. Both chambers are located at the Palace of Westminster (also simply called Westminster).

The House of Commons contained 646 elected Members of Parliament (or, MPs for short) after the 2005 general election. The government must convince a majority of these MPs to give their support in order to pass a new law. The new law is then considered by the House of Lords, which may ask for alterations or even withhold approval.

Spreading the power

Parliament has governed for centuries from the Palace of Westminster. However, several years ago, major changes were made to parliament, in a process known as devolution. Certain powers were devolved (passed on) to two new chambers—a Scottish parliament in Edinburgh and a Welsh assembly in Cardiff—in order to give Scotland and Wales more influence over the running of their own affairs. (Amid some difficulty, devolution has also been attempted in Northern Ireland.)

In practice, devolution means that many issues exclusive to these countries can be dealt with locally, instead of in London. Some people see devolution as a stepping-stone to full Scottish and Welsh independence from the UK.

"England is the mother of parliaments."

JOHN BRIGHT (1811–89),
BRITISH STATESMAN

The queen, as head of state, opens parliament in an elaborate ceremony every November.

The European question

The UK is a member state of the European Union (EU), and this, too, involves the British government giving up some of its power. Certain laws, especially relating to trade, are passed by the European parliament in Strasbourg and Brussels, and applied across the EU. In return, all 25 EU members can easily export their goods to one another.

Some British people believe Europe has too much influence. The UK chose not to adopt the European single currency, known as the euro. And the extent to which the country should allow the EU to control its affairs has become a highly charged political question.

Pomp and power: the state opening of parliament

Each session of the British parliament is opened in a ceremony led by the Queen. Dressed in majestic robes, she arrives at Westminster in a horse-drawn carriage. Politicians and invited guests assemble in the House of Lords to hear her deliver a speech. The speech has been prepared by ministers, and outlines the government's agenda. The event is full of historic rituals. For example, a government official is held at Buckingham Palace as a symbolic hostage for the monarch's safe return, echoing the days when monarchs and elected politicians vied with each other for power.

History: Forging the nation

The British nation grew out of the union of England Scotland, and Wales, and the story of its development is one of war, trade, and religious solidarity.

Wales incorporated

Britain's formal unification is relatively recent, stretching back only a few centuries. The first so-called Act of Union was passed in 1536, during the reign of King Henry VIII, and began the integration of Wales into England. At that time most of Wales was already under the control of the English king. But Henry had just declared himself leader of the Church of England, thwarting the power of the Catholic Pope, based in Rome. Worried that forces loyal to the Pope might use Wales as a springboard to invade England, he decided to increase his control over it. The semi-independent border estates, known as the Welsh Marches, were converted into counties, and were represented in the English parliament. Then, all of Wales was made subject to English law, and English was made the main language, with the native Welsh tongue relegated to second-class status.

Troubled union

In 1707, another Act of Union was passed by the parliaments of England and Scotland. This replaced both bodies with a single British parliament, based in London, and created the United Kingdom of Great Britain. England and Scotland had different reasons for uniting. The English wanted to prevent a Scottish Catholic from becoming king, while the Scottish wanted to gain access to English colonies and the more powerful English economy. The Scots were also granted considerable financial incentives to unite. And, to further accommodate them, the Scottish Church and legal system were left in place. But many ordinary people were still opposed to the union.

A key factor holding the United Kingdom together throughout the eighteenth century was the need to oppose the armies of Roman Catholic France. This painting shows the French victory at the Battle of Denain in 1712.

Britannia: Beauty and power personified

Britannia was the Romans' name for their colony in Britain. It was represented on coins by the figure of a goddesslike woman. This human image of Britain was revived in the eighteenth century (right) to celebrate the new nation, and has survived to this day. Britannia holds a trident and a shield, and is usually depicted in robes and a helmet. The British lion often sits at her feet, which are lapped by waves, symbolizing Britain's naval power.

Common interest

After 1707, the idea of a common British identity gained strength only because each country could see the benefits in it. In particular, they were all enriched by advantages of having an empire in the eighteenth and nineteenth centuries. And continuous military threats from Catholic Europe—especially France—knit the Protestant UK ever closer together.

In 1801, yet another Act of Union brought the Irish into the UK, again in response to fears of invasion, though in the twentieth century, most of Ireland became an independent republic. Today, of course, neither the invasion fears nor the empire exist. As a result, a minority of people have begun to question the need to call themselves British, as opposed to English, Scottish, Welsh, or Irish.

TIMELINE: THE QUEST FOR UNITY

1534: Act of Supremacy makes King Henry VIII head of the Church of England

1536-43: Acts of Union incorporate Wales into England

1603: James VI of Scotland inherits the English throne. Rules as James I of England

1607: Unsuccessful attempt by James I to formalize a union between Scotland and England

1707: Act of Union between England and Scotland creates a unified British state

1793: Start of wars against revolutionary France

1801: Act of Union with Ireland

1921: Irish Free State established (later the Republic of Ireland). Northern Ireland remains part of the UK

"We are no longer kept together by the need to fight wars, we are no longer all Protestants, and we do not have the self-interest of belonging to a massive global empire."

LINDA COLLEY, BRITISH HISTORIAN, 1992

History: Empire and industry

The British became the most powerful and wealthy nation in the world, thanks to a combination of technical ingenuity and military might.

Industrial revolution

In 1815, the UK's defeat of its greatest enemy, France, at the Battle of Waterloo, enabled British colonial influence to spread around the globe unchallenged. By the late nineteenth century, one quarter of the world's people lived within the British Empire. Over the same period, the UK economy was transformed. Central to this was the development of an efficient steam engine by Scotsman, James Watt (1736–1819), in the late eighteenth century. Small-scale manufacturing—already expanding—now grew more rapidly than ever. Big steam-powered factories churned out iron goods, textiles, and other products that had previously been made by people working from home. Steam also powered railroads and ships, allowing goods to be transported more easily. The massive British Empire provided cheap raw materials for UK industry, as well as a place for the UK to sell its manufactured goods.

The Industrial Revolution's advances in industry, such as the iron-making shown here, helped the UK become a world power.

A nation enslaved

British industrial and imperial riches did not, however, go unnoticed. In the nineteenth century, Germany emerged as a new European rival, seeking to compete with the UK in a hostile rivalry. This eventually led to the horrors of World War I.

But even during peacetime, the industrial revolution had drawbacks. It could provide higher-paid jobs than those in agriculture, but it often condemned the workers to long hours in the brutal conditions of the factories. And giant, ugly cities, full of chimneys belching smoke and terrible slums, scarred the landscape. For decades until the introduction of limited reforms in the Victorian era, many poorer Britons must have felt more like victims of their country's success, not its beneficiaries.

Sugar Trade.

The slave trade

One of the more unsavory aspects of British economic development was the slave trade. Millions of Africans were shipped from their homes to the Americas and forced to work as servants in houses or laborers in the fields and on plantations. Often, they were exchanged for products like cotton, which were sold back in Britain or turned into manufactured goods, to buy yet more slaves. Port cities like Liverpool and Bristol grew fabulously wealthy on the proceeds, and some historians believe slavery underpinned the UK's early industrial growth.

> "In the best cases a temporarily endurable existence...in the worst cases, bitter want, reaching even homelessness and death by starvation."
> FRIEDRICH ENGELS (1820-1895), GERMAN POLITICAL PHILOSOPHER, COMMENTING ON THE ENGLISH INDUSTRIAL WORKING CLASS IN 1844

Service economy

Since then, the UK economy has undergone a second revolution. Because of foreign competition, heavy industries, such as coal mining and shipbuilding, all but disappeared in the late twentieth century. Manufacturing has diminished considerably as well, and today, more Britons than ever work in the service industries like finance, retailing, and leisure.

Some people argue these types of jobs are less secure than the ones they have replaced. But they are generally much cleaner, and safer too. And thanks in part to the lead it established more than 200 years ago, the United Kingdom remains one of the world's biggest exporters of both goods and services.

TIMELINE: THE RISE OF EMPIRE AND INDUSTRY

1712:	First commercially successful steam engine built by Thomas Newcomen. Used to pump water out of coal mines
1763:	Britain and her allies defeat the French in North America
1772:	Extensive canal building begins
1775:	James Watt's improved steam engine
1783:	Loss of Britain's American colonies
1805:	Battle of Trafalgar: Britain gains naval supremacy after defeating the French
1812:	First "Luddite" riots: impoverished artisans sabotage machinery
1815:	Defeat of Napoleon at Battle of Waterloo
1830:	World's first passenger railroad opens between Liverpool and Manchester
1846:	Repeal of Corn Laws introduces free trade
1851:	The Great Exhibition: the UK shows off its world lead in manufacturing

England

England is the UK's dominant country in terms of population and economic might. But few people seem to know what it really means to be English.

English—or British?

One explanation is that the English, as leading players in Britain, have plowed their self-respect into a wider British nationality instead. Today, that may be changing, as the UK becomes less centralized and each country takes more control of its own affairs. Some English people observe nationalism in Northern Ireland, Scotland, and Wales, and want to respond by strengthening their own separate cultural identity. Others complain that they pay more in tax and receive less government spending than the rest of the UK. Now, for the first time in centuries, the flag of Saint George has become popular again. The English may at last be stirring. And some people fear that a more assertive England could spell problems for the smaller countries of the UK.

North–South divide

More than three quarters of all UK citizens live in England, but the country is so regionally diverse that some inhabitants can look upon others as virtual foreigners. Accents, attitudes, and even lifestyles can differ greatly. One popular stereotype is that those from the south tend to think of themselves as cultured and refined, while northerners are more likely to be working class. There may be little truth in this, but it stems from the undeniable fact that most heavy industry in England was based in the urban midlands and north, while London and the southeast have traditionally formed a wealthier political and administrative region. Today the north–south economic divide remains a matter for some concern. Meanwhile, the east and west of England are overwhelmingly rural.

Two English city stereotypes: the leafy suburban south and the grim industrial north. In reality there is wealth and poverty in both areas and, recently, northern cities have become prosperous after decades of industrial decline.

Defining the English identity

Despite the struggle to find a single identity, there are some cultural traits the English like to think of as their own. These include a notion of fair play, as enshrined in the typically English game of cricket, an ability to laugh at oneself, and a cool, reserved personality.

In 2006 a government-sponsored poll found that the most popular symbols of England included the FA Cup, Punch and Judy, and a cup of tea, although—characteristically—many English people had different ideas about their country. Meanwhile, the rich English language lends itself to poetry and prose, and there is justifiable celebration of literary giants such as Shakespeare. Yet few people seem to display much obvious pride in being English. The commemoration of the national patron saint, Saint George's Day, is not even a civic holiday.

Is this how the rest of the world sees England? In a recent survey people listed a cup of tea as being symbolic of English culture.

Morris dance: a curious custom

Few things better display English eccentricity than the traditional Morris dance. Dancers (often men, although there are women Morris dancers) leap and step in formation to folk music. They wear bright costumes with bells on their legs, twirl handkerchiefs, and clatter wooden sticks together. Morris dancing possibly originated as a celebration of springtime, or even as ritualized combat.

Scotland

The most northerly country in Great Britain looks warily on its southern neighbor England, and prides itself on being different.

Rugged beauty

In many ways Scotland feels like a big country, with its breathtaking landscape of mountains, lochs and far-flung islands. Only 8.5% of British people are Scottish but they are a proud and fiercely individual people. Living so far north, the climate they experience is often harsh by UK standards, and the people have developed a reputation for being just as tough as their weather. Even the Romans, who invaded Britain in the first century C.E., were unable to subdue the Scots. In fact, the Roman emperor Hadrian had to build a giant wall to keep the Scots out of his colony to the south.

A view of the skyline of the Scottish capital Edinburgh.

Anything but English

Today, the Scots are once again asserting themselves, albeit peacefully. A nationalist minority believes Scotland's future lies in independence from the rest of the United Kingdom. But even those who support the Union love nothing better than getting the better of their old rivals, the English— especially on the soccer or rugby field. Such sparring, though, is generally good humored. In fact, according to tradition, the Scots are committed to social justice to an extent not seen anywhere else in the UK. They have a separate legal and educational system, while the Scottish parliament has tended toward more generous health and welfare policies than those available south of the border.

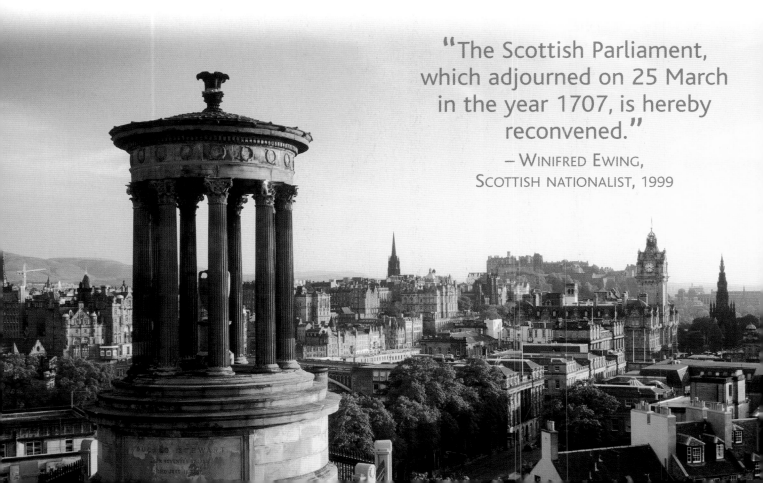

"The Scottish Parliament, which adjourned on 25 March in the year 1707, is hereby reconvened."

— WINIFRED EWING,
SCOTTISH NATIONALIST, 1999

Scottish Highland scenery includes mountains, lochs (lakes) and heather-covered hills.

Work ethic

The Scots are also known for being particularly hardworking and shrewd, with very noticeable talents for science and engineering. Perhaps it is no surprise then that this is the country that produced the inventors of television and the telephone and, just recently, the scientists who first cloned an animal, Dolly the sheep. Scots also gained a reputation as able colonial administrators in the days of the British Empire.

To many people, though, Scotland means bagpipes, the Highland Games, Hogmanay (New Year), and whiskey. With such a strong and distinctive culture, it is easy to think of the country as a single, indivisible unit. But there are differences within Scottish society, too. In particular, some people in the remote highlands and islands are as wary of Scotland's urban elite as Scots may be of the English!

Burns: Scottish hero

Robert Burns (above), who lived from 1759 to 1796, is the best known of the Scots-language poets, penning such classics as Auld Lang Syne and Tam O'Shanter. A political radical, his works often celebrated the weak and vulnerable in a Scotland that he also depicted as the underdog. Today he remains as a symbol of Scottish culture. His birthday, January 25, is known as Burns Night. Scots mark it to this day with the ritual "Burns Supper," with readings, toasts, and haggis (ground sheep's organ meats and oatmeal in a casing).

Wales (Cymru)

Wales has been subject to continuous rule from London for more than 800 years, but its spirit and customs still flourish.

Caernarfon Castle was one of the many fortresses built by the English king, Edward I, when he conquered Wales.

Ancient and modern

Wales is steeped in history. Its mountainous terrain is peppered with mighty castles dating back to the thirteenth century, when the English King Edward I conquered the country. Yet the Welsh are also a forward-looking people, with renewed self-confidence. Around one fifth of them now speak Welsh, which is taught along with English in schools. Most road signs are bilingual, and there is also Welsh-language broadcasting. The Welsh cultural year reaches its climax in the National Eisteddfod, a Welsh-language literary and arts festival held each August.

Hard times

Life in Wales, though, has sometimes been tough. Most of the population lives in the south, where iron and coal deposits fueled the growth of heavy industry in the nineteenth century. These areas were then hit hard by economic downturn. Today, almost all the coal mines and heavy industry have gone, and the country has had to diversify into areas like electronics, oil refining, and tourism. Meanwhile, much Welsh agricultural land is of relatively poor quality, and suitable only for raising sheep and cattle. The country lies in the path of westerly winds from the Atlantic, making the climate cool and damp.

Quest for justice

Thanks in part to this historic adversity, Welsh people have often been wary of the rich and powerful. They have tended to vote for politicians who support social justice and to follow nonconformist religions like Methodism, which reject pomp and ceremony in favor of more simple worship. One of the most famous Welsh members of parliament was Aneurin Bevan, who, as the British Health Minister in the 1940s, helped establish the UK's National Health Service.

Since 1999, an assembly has sat in the Welsh capital, Cardiff. But, unlike the Scottish parliament, it does not have the power to raise taxes. The Welsh nationalist party, Plaid Cymru, would like to upgrade the assembly, and make Wales an independent country.

Welsh MP Aneurin Bevan, part-founder of the UK's National Health Service in 1948.

"Every day when I wake up I thank the Lord I'm Welsh."

CERYS MATTHEWS,
WELSH POP SINGER, 1998

Cool Cymru

Wales entered the twenty-first century on an upbeat, thanks to the creation of its devolved assembly but also to an explosion of culture known as Cool Cymru. Led by successful bands such as the Manic Street Preachers and the Stereophonics, it has lit up a country long overshadowed by its English neighbor. And the new Millennium Stadium in Cardiff has given Welsh rugby a spectacular home.

The Manic Street Preachers on stage in Swansea.

Northern Ireland

Northern Ireland—the biggest part of the UK to lie outside Great Britain—offers some spectacular scenery. Its people are trying to overcome the legacies of decades of conflict.

Scenic wonder

Northern Ireland was formed out of six counties of Ireland that did not join the Irish Free State in 1921. Like the rest of Ireland it is largely rural, and known for its landscape. At its center is a huge lake called Lough Neagh—the largest in the UK. And a spectacular volcanic rock formation called the Giant's Causeway graces the north coast. But despite the beauty of its land, Northern Ireland's recent history has been a difficult one.

Northern Ireland includes some of the UK's most spectacular scenery. The Giant's Causeway, shown here, is a UNESCO World Heritage Site.

Sectarian terror

The problems are often expressed in religious terms, but they really concern Northern Ireland's links with Great Britain. Part of the population is descended from Scottish and English settlers who colonized the region several hundred years ago. These people are overwhelmingly Protestant in faith and see themselves as British. But the remainder of Northern Ireland is Catholic, and wants to belong to the Republic of Ireland.

Paramilitary extremists from the two rival communities unleashed campaigns of violence in the 1970s, which came to be known as the Troubles. Over the next three decades, more than 3,600 people died as a result.

Optimism and obstacles

Today, the Troubles are in effect over, after the main anti-British paramilitary group, the IRA, declared a ceasefire and committed its followers to politics instead. As a result, the economy has boomed. Tourism and business, once scared away, have begun to return. Northern Ireland's inhabitants can now choose to be British or Irish citizens, or both. And provision has been made for a devolved assembly to sit at Stormont Castle in Belfast.

But challenges remain. Unemployment is higher than most parts of the UK, and some urban districts remain squalid and uninviting. A number of former paramilitaries have moved into organized crime. And there has been little agreement among politicians on how to move forward. Northern Ireland may no longer be at war with itself, but the transition to a peaceful, settled society will take time.

Sinn Féin leader Gerry Adams (center) speaks to the media about the Good Friday Agreement in 1998.

> "The leadership has formally ordered an end to the armed campaign."
>
> IRA STATEMENT, JULY 2005

The peace process

The Good Friday Agreement of 1998 paved the way to a devolved assembly where Catholics and Protestants can share power. Northern Ireland is now linked to both the Irish Republic and the UK, but with neither country claiming the province as its own. Instead, Northern Ireland's future is to be decided by a majority of its own people.

Paramilitary prisoners have been released from jail, and there have been reforms to policing and security. But some Protestant politicians have criticized the Agreement, saying they are not satisfied that the IRA has given up armed struggle for ever.

Offshore neighbors

Some parts of the British Isles are neither fully independent, nor fully British. The Channel Islands and the Isle of Man are ancient realms with unusual links to the mainland.

Semidetached

The Channel Islands, just off the French coast, are leftovers of the period long ago when English kings ruled over the French region of Normandy, and their status reflects this complex history. The islands are crown dependencies, meaning that the British queen is head of state, although she rules under the title Duke of Normandy, and islanders are entitled to be British citizens. However, the islands themselves are neither part of the United Kingdom, nor members of the European Union. And they are mostly free to form their own treaties with foreign countries, because the UK government only has authority over major issues such as defense.

Tax haven

There are five main inhabited Channel islands: Jersey, Guernsey, Alderney, Sark, and Herm. Although they share a TV station, almost everything else is done separately, each island having its own legislature, laws, and elections. On Sark, decisions are taken by Europe's last remaining feudal overlord, known as the Seigneur. Cars are banned there, while on the even smaller island of Herm, bicycles too are prohibited.

But the islands are perhaps best known for having extremely low rates of income tax, and they have become home to a flourishing banking industry, as well as to those seeking to avoid UK taxes. In order to prevent these people from outnumbering locals, outsiders are only allowed to buy the most expensive properties. Therefore most Britons only see the Channel Islands when taking part in their other big economic activity, which is tourism.

St. Peter Port, the capital of Guernsey, is a popular destination for sailing small boats.

A step back in time

Another tax refuge with similar relations with the UK is the Isle of Man. Located in the Irish Sea around 60 miles from the western coast of Britain, it is a historic treasure. Horse-drawn trams carry people around the capital, Douglas, while elsewhere a steam railroad operates, and the parliament, known as the Tynwald, dates back more than a thousand years, making it possibly the oldest continuous assembly in the world.

Manx culture is much influenced by the island's Viking and Celtic roots, and the local language, similar to Gaelic, is once again being taught after all but dying out. The Isle of Man also boasts some unique, curious animals including the four-horned "loaghtan" sheep and the tailless Manx cat.

The TT: festival of speed

Life offshore isn't all about avoiding UK tax. The Isle of Man TT is a series of thrilling motorcycle races held every summer (right). Riders compete at up to 125 mph (200 km/h) on a course around the island's winding lanes, which are closed to all other traffic. The event attracts up to 40,000 spectators, and also includes many social activities.

The main inhabited offshore dependencies + area (in sq miles/km) & pop (2003)

Jersey	45/116	87,186	UK dependency
Guernsey	24/62	59,807	UK dependency
Herm	0.7/2	60	Guernsey dependency
Sark	2/5	600	Guernsey dependency
Alderney	2/5	2400	Guernsey dependency
Isle of Man	220/572	76,315	UK dependency

London: The UK's world city

The English and UK capital is Europe's biggest city and one of the most exciting on Earth. But it is also a city of surprises and challenges.

Center and suburbs

London is actually two cities in one: the "Square Mile" of the original City of London, which is now the capital's financial district, and the bigger City of Westminster next door to it—home to the queen at Buckingham Palace. Around these two centers, another 31 boroughs sprawl. Since 2000 the whole metropolis of more than seven million people has been partly self-governed by an elected mayor and an assembly that sits at a brand new City Hall, near Tower Bridge.

Economic giant

London is the center of England's legal, media, and, of course, political establishments. It is also its economic powerhouse. It is so strong economically that some people worry that other parts of the country risk being sidelined. London's historic role as a merchant center is now reflected in the billions of pounds worth of currency traded daily in the square mile.

London is ideally suited as a hub for trade because, being located at the center of global time—the Greenwich Meridian—its working day overlaps with both North America and the Far East. After hours, the city becomes a major entertainment center. Its famous theater district, the West End, also boasts top-class restaurants, nightclubs, and bars. Today in London you can hear speak more than 300 different languages, so it is no surprise that the city has an international flavor.

An evening view of part of the City of London from the south bank of the Thames River with Blackfriars Bridge in the foreground. The dome of St. Paul's Cathedral still dominates the City skyline, just as it did when completed by architect Sir Christopher Wren in 1709. Other tall buildings visible are Tower 42 (center right) and the Swiss-Re building, known popularly as "The Gherkin" (far right).

"When a man is tired of London, he is tired of life; for there is in London all that life can afford."
SAMUEL JOHNSON (1709–1784), ENGLISH EIGHTEENTH-CENTURY ESSAYIST

The hidden side

Despite its size and power though, the capital is in many ways a collection of urban villages. Many small neighborhoods such as Soho and Notting Hill retain an intimate charm, and between them, vast parks offer relief from the noise and traffic. Yet visitors to London might be even more surprised to discover, alongside all the wealth, areas of great poverty too.

Crime, drugs, and other social problems blight some districts. And for many people, buying their own home in this expensive city is out of the question. Add to this an aging transit system, and London's challenges become apparent. One solution might be the Olympic Games, to be held in London in 2012. The authorities hope this momentous event will spark widespread regeneration, especially in run-down eastern areas of the city.

Ken Livingstone: London's first elected mayor

As brash and outspoken as London itself, Ken Livingstone (below) became the first person to occupy the newly created post of mayor in 2000. Previously known as Red Ken for his left-wing views, he championed minorities and the poor—often at the expense of more wealthy citizens. His many other controversies include attempting to free Trafalgar Square of its famous pigeons and introducing a so-called congestion charge (see page 32 for details of how it works). But supporters still felt Mr. Livingstone reflected the spirit of London.

Town and country

The UK is densely populated, and changes in the patterns of living are putting a great strain on town and countryside alike—especially in England.

Rush to the countryside

For several decades now, many of England's big towns and cities have been shrinking as hundreds of thousands of people leave for the countryside, hoping for a better quality of life. In particular, almost every one of the past 35 years have seen a drift toward the wealthier southeast of the country, and the effects of such movements have been dramatic. Some older industrial towns are in decline, as their better-off inhabitants move out. While the government is having to plan thousands of new homes elsewhere to accommodate the shifting population—even in areas protected against development, known as green belt. Already, across England, many once-rural areas have become home to newly developed suburbs, roads, and giant "out-of-town" shopping malls.

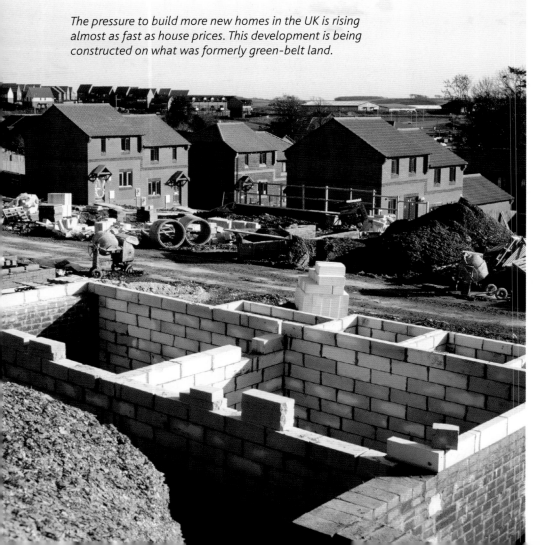

The pressure to build more new homes in the UK is rising almost as fast as house prices. This development is being constructed on what was formerly green-belt land.

Rural crisis

These trends have coincided with a decline in agriculture, with the result that the rural way of life is changing fast. Some people fear that traditional villages risk becoming mere bedroom communities, which are empty by day as their new inhabitants commute to work in nearby cities. Many small businesses such as farms and local village stores have closed. Rural post offices have also been shut down. And when in 2005 the government banned the traditional country sport of hunting foxes with hounds, many critics began to claim that the traditional country way of life was going to disappear forever.

Developing problems

The government wants to meet rising demand for housing in the southeast of England by allowing up to a million new homes to be built there. Many, such as those shown in the picture on the right, will be subsidized so that vital workers such as nurses and teachers can afford to live in them. And most will not be built on rural land. But the plans have unleashed a storm of criticism. Campaigners argue that there will not be enough transportation, power, or even water for all the new residents. They say the plans will leave a concrete scar across the countryside.

"England could lose most of its real countryside within a single generation."

CAMPAIGN TO PROTECT RURAL ENGLAND, 2005

Planning for change

Today, the challenge is to accommodate change without altering the face of England—and the rest of the UK—forever. Some people think organic farming could help save cash-strapped farmers. Others claim the countryside must diversify into providing leisure facilities, or growing new crops. Meanwhile, a number of rural authorities have introduced laws to stop outsiders snapping up scarce local property.

There may be some relief in store from the rush to populate the countryside as efforts are being made to improve run-down cities. Converting old, disused industrial buildings into fashionable apartments and lofts seems to be paying off, and after many years, living in the city might once again be considered a desirable alternative.

ENGLAND'S HOUSING CRISIS:

Surplus housing supply, 1999 (available dwellings over households needing accommodation)

Northern England: 3.0%
Midlands: 2.2%
South: 0.9%
London: -2.2%

Expected rise in number of households needing accommodation, 2001-2021:

Northern England: 8.8% (539,000 new households)
Midlands: 12.1% (478,000 new households)
South: 18.9% (1,400,000 new households)
London: 16.5% (517,000 new households)

Transportation: Jam tomorrow

With so many people and so little land, getting around is becoming one of the UK's most difficult problems.

Legacy of neglect

For decades, British governments failed to spend enough money on the nation's transportation infrastructure. Today, travelers are paying the price. Unlike most European countries, trains, buses, and subways in the UK can be unreliable, despite charging some of the highest fares in the world. The railroad network —the world's oldest—is only just recovering from a spate of serious accidents, some caused by rail companies neglecting to maintain the tracks. Even so the government is working hard to move even more people and freight off the roads and onto rail. Since 1994, it has had considerable success in doing so.

Clearing the way

Despite this, the roads themselves remain stretched to capacity. Building new ones has become unpopular for environmental reasons. But car ownership has risen steeply across the United Kingdom. In response, the government is planning to lure drivers back onto other forms of transportation, using satellite technology to track vehicle movements and charge a fee for each mile driven. In London, drivers already pay a flat fee to enter the city center at peak times, which has substantially reduced traffic. But politicians elsewhere fear that monitoring drivers' trips and pricing them out of their cars may be unpopular, so other cities have been slow to adopt their own charging schemes.

Back to the future

One solution to the UK's transportation crisis is the reintroduction of trolleys (above), some 50 years after most cities scrapped them. Less expensive to build than a subway and faster than a bus, the trolley has the added advantages of being clean, quiet, and pleasing to the eye. Manchester, Sheffield, and Croydon are among the places that use trolleys. Dozens of other places are also considering the idea.

The pressure on airports to expand has increased dramatically in the last two decades, mirroring the demand for cheap air travel. Campaigners worry that the enlargement of airports like Stansted, in Essex, will destroy the countryside forever.

The sky's limits

Surprisingly perhaps, one of the cheapest ways to travel now in the UK can be to fly. Thanks to the emergence of budget carriers, it is possible to fly off for just a few dollars. Some Britons even have second homes overseas, which they commute to every weekend. But the growth in air travel has its own problems. For instance, London is now served by no fewer than five airports, yet even more capacity is needed to meet expected demand. And expanding airports is deeply controversial. Supporters say the UK's economic future depends on it. But critics point out the destruction of countryside and increased environmental damage. It seems that, for now at least, even the skies over the United Kingdom are doomed to suffer traffic jams.

> "We inherited a creaking transport system: Congested roads and overcrowded trains."
>
> JOHN PRESCOTT,
> DEPUTY PRIME MINISTER,
> JULY 2000

FACTFILE: TRANSPORTATION

ROADS (Great Britain)
Expressways: 2,704 miles (4,353 km)
Major roads: 34,745 miles (55,918 km)
Minor roads: 140,168 miles (225,579 km)
Number of vehicles registered (2001):
29.7 million
Total road-traffic growth (2004): 1.7%
Estimated road-traffic growth by 2040: 40%

RAILROADS (Great Britain)
Total rail network: 10,275 miles (16,536 km)
Amount electrified: 3,062 miles (4,928 km)
Passenger miles traveled (2004): 25.8 billion
Journeys made per day (2004): 2,820,000

AIR
Number of passengers (2002): 189 million
Number of passengers predicted (2030):
476 million
Average growth per year: 4.25%
Number of foreign vacations taken by UK residents per year: 41 million

OTHER
Average number of bicycle trips per person per year (2004): 15
Average bicycle miles/km traveled per person per year (2004): 36/58
Average distance walked per person per year (2001): 189 miles (304 km)

Health: The costs of living

The UK was at the forefront of twentieth-century health and welfare provision, but today, it is having to change the way it looks after itself.

Inside a privately run hospital. More and more people with health problems choose to "go private," instead of waiting for treatment on the National Health Service.

The state steps in

After World War II, the British government introduced an extensive welfare system, which provided free care for everyone, regardless of income, from the cradle to the grave. The crowning glory of this so-called welfare state was the National Health Service (NHS), where even the poorest citizens could see a doctor and get treatment. The NHS has since become one of the nation's best-loved institutions— and one of the most expensive. In the year 2005, for example, it cost $155 billion to run.

Plugging the gap

One problem is that the UK's people are now living longer than ever before. This means the cost of medicines and operations is rising, as more patients grow old and frail. Today, with a huge investment program underway, more taxpayers' money than ever is being spent on the NHS. But even this is not enough. So the Service is trying to find the extra funds needed by teaming up with private companies to build new hospitals and even to provide some treatments. Not everyone approves of the idea, because they are so attached to the NHS and fear that introducing profit-making companies into the system may weaken its basic principle of being free to use.

Putting on weight: the UK's fat problem

The UK is better than ever at treating the unwell, but in some respects it is still becoming more unhealthy. Obesity (as in picture, right) has tripled in the last 20 years, thanks to more car use, richer food, and fewer people doing heavy manual work. By 2010, one quarter of all adults could be dangerously overweight, spelling up to $8 billion in additional health costs. Obese people are more likely to develop heart disease, diabetes, and high blood pressure.

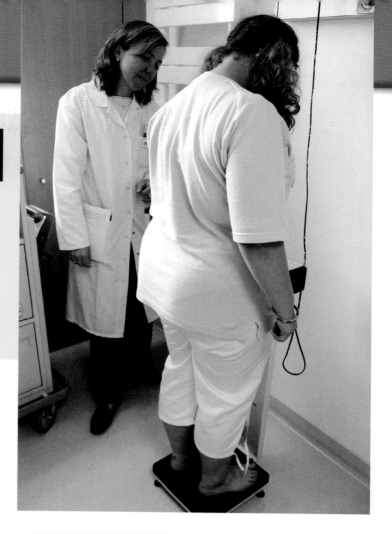

"We expect more from our health care system than ever."

HEALTH THINK-TANK, THE KING'S FUND, 2004

Prevention not cure

At the same time, the health authorities are trying to encourage people to look after themselves better and not to get sick in the first place. They have introduced measures to encourage more healthy eating habits, and—because only a minority of Britons now smoke—to ban smoking in public places.

Alcohol abuse, too, has become a big issue. One third of British men and one-fifth of women drink more than they should, and 22,000 people a year die because of alcohol-related illnesses.

Alcohol abuse causes other problems, too. For example, many people get involved in crimes and violence through being drunk. The government is especially worried about alcohol abuse among young people. But one of its solutions—to extend the hours in which alcohol can be consumed in pubs, bars, and clubs—is proving controversial. Ministers believe it encourages people to drink more slowly and responsibly. But opponents worry that it will lead to a massive increase in consumption, and even more illness.

FACTFILE : HEALTH —COSTS AND BENEFITS ($US)

NHS spending (1997-8):	$88 billion
NHS spending (2005-6):	$155 billion
Projected NHS spending (2007-8):	$190 billion

Number of NHS employees	1,300,000
Average cost of a doctor (2004-5)	$170,000pa
Average cost of a nurse (2004-5)	$50,000pa
NHS funding deficit (2005-6):	$1.2 billion

Waiting list for hospital treatment (1997):
1,158,000
Waiting list for hospital treatment (2004):
857,000

In 2003-04 the NHS provided:-
- 325 million consultations with doctors or nurses
- 13.3 million outpatient consultations
- 5.4 million planned hospital admissions
- 4.2 million emergency hospital admissions

Leisure: Tradition and adventure

The UK's favorite pastime is, unsurprisingly, watching television. But beyond that, the nation enjoys a wealth of recreation.

Staying home

Most people in the UK work a five-day week, Monday to Friday, so weekends are the main time for entertainment. This trend may even have increased in recent years, because the laws restricting store openings on Sundays have been relaxed. Yet, in this house-proud land, the home, as well as the public sphere, is a major leisure arena. A recent EU survey found that the most popular pursuit after watching TV is visiting friends to eat and drink. Other domestic activities include gardening and carrying out home improvements.

> "All work and no play makes Jack a dull boy."
> ENGLISH PROVERB

New tastes

When people do go out, many still visit that unique British institution, the public house, or pub. The pub is a place for talking to strangers, getting to know the owner, and playing games or even sports. Pub-going though is facing competition. For one thing, the UK has discovered food. Scores of different cuisines are now available in almost any big town or city. Such is the fondness for Indian food, for example, that a popular variety of curry was recently voted as the UK's true national dish.

In the field of culture, the movies are the biggest attraction, but theater, dance, and live music also draw in the crowds. And visits to public art galleries and museums have almost doubled since the government abolished entrance fees, several years ago. The arts benefit from grants provided by the UK National Lottery.

The British public house has traditionally been at the heart of a neighborhood; a place for socializing as well as drinking.

Rugby is one of UK's most popular sports for TV viewing. For participating though, walking comes out on top.

On the field

The pastime about which the UK is perhaps the most passionate of all, however, is sport. Soccer and rugby are played in all four countries, while in England and some parts of Wales, cricket also predominates in summer. England's 2003 rugby world cup triumph, and its victory over the Australians in the 2005 cricket series, have boosted interest in both. And it is hoped that the Olympic Games, to be held in London in 2012, will boost participation in sports more generally.

The BBC: broadcasting legend

The British Broadcasting Corporation, or BBC, is one of the world's largest providers of radio, television and internet content. Dating back to 1922, it began the first-ever regular TV service in 1936, and its programs are still seen as among the best. They are also free of commercials—free because the BBC is funded by a yearly license that, by law, all television owners must buy.

A staunchly independent news-provider, BBC journalists have attracted the displeasure of British and foreign governments alike.

FACTFILE: LEISURE

Average time spent watching television each day:
Males: 2 hours 45 minutes
Females: 2 hours 25 minutes

Average time spent doing housework each day:
Males: 1 hour 40 minutes
Females: 3 hours

Visits to the movies (2004): 171 million
Number of households with internet access (2005): 12.9 million

Top tourist attractions, 2001 (with visitor numbers in millions)
Blackpool pleasure beach (6.5); National Gallery, London (4.9); British Museum, London (4.8); Tate Modern art gallery, London (3.6); Tower of London (2.0); York Minster, York, and Legoland, Windsor (1.6 each)

Most popular sports (with percentage of adults taking part)
Walking/rambling (70); Swimming (27); Keep fit (23); Snooker/pool (19); Biking (18); Weight training (12); Fishing (11); Soccer (10)

Education: Put to the test

Education is changing rapidly in the UK today, as the government aims to provide a better education for more youngsters. But not everyone agrees on the best way to do this.

Top class

Not all UK schools are the same. Some, known as public schools, are in fact privately run; they receive little or no government money, and parents pay fees instead. However, most children attend a state-funded school.

Today, these are changing, because the government wants schools to have more control over their own affairs. Failing schools, for example, can be closed and replaced by schools with the support of local businesses, or religious and community groups. Critics say the sponsors get too much influence over what children are taught. But ministers say they bring specialist knowledge and help provide brand new facilities at a lower cost to taxpayers.

The schools system has been a top priority of recent UK governments.

Paying to learn

The schooling and exam system differs in England and Wales, Scotland, and Northern Ireland. At age 18 though, a growing number of children throughout the UK now go to college or university. This normally involves moving away from home for the first time. In recent years, studying at university has become much more expensive. Many students do not receive a grant to cover living expenses, and also have to pay some of their tuition fees. Special government loans are available to cover these costs. The loans do not have to be repaid until the student has graduated and begun work.

> "Ask me my three main priorities for government, and I tell you: education, education, education."
>
> TONY BLAIR,
> BRITISH PRIME MINISTER-TO-BE,
> OCTOBER, 1996

EDUCATION FACT FILE:

Enrollments to higher education courses (2002-3): 2,175,115 (up 4.3%)

MIXED ACHIEVEMENTS:
Percentage of qualified work force by region (2003)
Which regions of the UK perform best?

	Degree or equiv.	High school or equiv.	None
UK as a whole	**16.3**	**21.7**	**15.0**
England / northeast	11.3	22.7	18.8
England / West Midlands	12.7	22.7	17.6
London	24.7	16.7	13.4
England / southeast	19.9	22.4	10.6
Wales	14.6	23.4	17.1
Scotland	15.4	16.4	14.7
Northern Ireland	13.1	21.0	23.7

THE BENEFITS OF LEARNING (2003 figures, $US)
Average income for employees qualified to degree level: $1,300pw
Average income for employees with no qualifications: $609pw
Number of adults qualified to degree level in full-time employment: 88%
Number of adults with no qualifications in full-time employment: 50%

The Open University

The UK's biggest university has no traditional campus and you don't need to pass any exams to get in. The Open University, established in the 1960s, aims to provide degree and post-graduate courses to anyone, regardless of their academic background. Students learn by attending seminars near where they live or work, and through specially made radio and TV programs. Many of them are older people who missed out on university when they left school. The university currently has around 150,000 undergraduates and 30,000 postgraduate students.

Could do better

By 2010, the government wants half of all students leaving school to continue studying at college or university. But media studies, psychology, and sociology are increasingly popular, while sciences and languages are often overlooked. Some business leaders believe today's graduates lack the skills that the UK needs, especially in areas like engineering and high technology. They argue that many young people would be better off taking vocational courses, apprenticeships, or simply starting work instead.

A pupil performs an experiment in a secondary-school laboratory. There is concern that not enough UK students choose science-based university courses.

Resources: Running on empty

For centuries, the UK has enjoyed food and energy to spare. But many of its natural resources are now growing more scarce.

Black gold

Compared to the rest of Europe, the UK has relatively little woodland and few mineral resources. However, few other countries on the continent have as much oil or gas to exploit. Huge lakes of oil beneath the North Sea were first tapped in 1975, and by the 1990s, the UK had become one of the world's top ten producers, producing up to one fifth of its own needs and generating impressive export revenues. Today, powerful rigs continue to drill the seabed off the shores of eastern Scotland, piping oil and natural gas back to the mainland. But this output has now reached its peak, and is expected to decline in years to come.

Future energy plans for the UK include the building of wind farms, such as the one shown here, to generate electricity as supplies of oil run out.

Renewable riches

The coal industry is already in decline, despite enormous reserves still lying beneath the British countryside. Cheap imports are mainly to blame, though demand is also falling because the government wants to encourage the use of cleaner forms of energy that do not contribute to global warming. Here, the UK's notoriously poor weather may come into its own, because there are plans to build huge wind farms. These will harness the power of nature to generate electricity. The waves lapping UK coastlines, too, may one day be used for this purpose. In the meantime, the government is considering a new generation of nuclear power stations to help fill the gap left by coal, oil, and gas.

The foot-and-mouth disease outbreak in 2001-2 resulted in thousands of animals having to be killed and burned.

Land of plenty?

The UK's edible resources, too, are facing problems. Around three quarters of the land is suitable for agriculture, and almost half of that can be used to grow crops. The best arable land is in southern and eastern England and eastern Scotland, while most of the rest can be used to keep livestock. Despite this, the UK imports almost half its food from abroad. And recent health scares such as foot-and-mouth disease and BSE (mad cow disease) have not helped its farmers.

Meanwhile the fishing industry, once stronger than most, is now facing ruin thanks to depleted fish stocks and stiff competition from European neighbors. It seems that, while the UK could once rely on natural resources for its wealth, in a less plentiful future it will instead have to look to its most promising asset of all for survival : the ideas and ingenuity of its people.

"An island of creativity surrounded by a sea of understanding."
Sir David Puttnam,
Government adviser, 1996

"An island of coal surrounded by a sea of fish."
Aneurin Bevan (1897–1960),
Government minister, 1945

FACTFILE: RESOURCES

Electricity production (2003):
From gas: 38%
From coal: 35%
From nuclear power: 22%
From oil: 1%
Others: 4%

Oil: Dwindling reserves, rising prices
Estimated reserves (and estimated value in $US)
2004: 3.0 bn tons   ($129bn)
2000: 3.8 bn tons   ($105.6 bn)
1995: 4.8 bn tons   ($79bn)

UK oil consumption: 1.76 million barrels per day (approx 74.5 million gallons)

Land use, millions of acres (1998):		
Developed land:	4.5	(7.7%)
Semi-natural land:	17	(29.8%)
Intensive agriculture:	26.6	(46%)
Woodland:	6.9	(11.9%)
Other:	2.7	(4.6%)

The UK tomorrow

The old certainties of empire, industry, and British national identity no longer hold true for the United Kingdom, and with their passing, the nation faces some daunting challenges.

Together or alone?

The UK faces many difficulties. Housing shortages, an outdated transportation system and environmental problems to name but a few. The biggest consideration though, may well be the political question of whether the United Kingdom continues to exist at all, or whether England, Scotland, Wales, and Northern Ireland decide at some future point to go their own separate ways. Some people believe that devolution has already started this process.

The other big political issue is the UK's place within the European Union. There is growing demand for the government to reject closer relations with other EU countries. But many businesses and pro-Europeans say the UK will find it difficult to survive unless it makes the most of these links.

Young and old

At home, the size and nature of the population is likely to pose some challenges too. With so many people living longer than ever before, health care and pensions will become a greater burden on the state. There is serious concern that younger people are not saving enough money now to pay for their own retirement. Meanwhile, the extent of immigration to the UK worries some people, while others say it is the only way to get the skilled and unskilled workers the economy needs. Without immigration, they add, there may not be enough taxpayers to meet the costs of the growing retired population.

One of the most hotly debated political issues in the UK today is greater integration within the EU, including the adoption of the Euro currency.

Working smarter

The kind of work people do is also likely to change. The UK will probably make fewer manufactured goods, and concentrate on providing services instead, so people will work with their brains rather than their hands.

Perhaps it is in this sphere that the best hopes lie, because the British are an original, inventive, and resourceful nation. In recent years they have proved they can turn away from dwelling on a glorious past and look to the future with confidence. In the United Kingdom today, the future may look tough. But the nation's record of energy, creativity, and open-mindedness suggests that, one way or another, it will continue to prosper.

The cost of health care to look after a population that is living longer will be a major social consideration in the United Kingdom's future.

FUTURE TRENDS: A CHANGING SOCIETY

Take a look at the following changes that took place over the 35 years between 1971 and 2003. What do they tell us about what kind of country the UK is likely to become in the future?

- The UK's population increased by 6% (3.6 million), but the number of separate households increased by 32%
- The number of people buying their own houses increased from 9.6 million to 18.1 million
- The average age of a UK citizen increased from 34.1 to 38.4
- Children living in lone-parent families tripled to 24%
- Male employment decreased from 92% to 79%, but female employment increased from 56% to 70%
- Spending on recreation and culture increased sixfold to $172 billion US
- The proportion of obese adults increased from 14.5% (in 1993) to 23% in 2003

Timeline of UK events

1066: William, Duke of Normandy, invades England and becomes king.

1170-5: English king, Henry II, conquers Ireland.

1282: Welsh prince Llywelyn defeated by English king, Edward I. Wales under English control.

1536: King Henry VIII passes Act of Union that makes Wales part of England.

1603: Queen Elizabeth I of England dies. James Stuart (King James VI of Scotland) becomes King James I of England and Scotland.

1642-59: Civil wars wreak havoc in England and Wales, Scotland, and Ireland. James's son, Charles I executed in 1649. England becomes a republic.

1660: Restoration of the monarchy. Charles II becomes king.

1688: Charles's Catholic brother James II gives up the throne. His Protestant daughter Mary and her husband William of Orange rule jointly.

1707: Act of Union under Mary's sister Queen Anne unites Scottish and English parliaments. The United Kingdom created.

1714: Queen Anne dies leaving no heirs; she is succeeded by her cousin George, Elector of Hanover, who becomes George I.

1715: Rebellion in Scotland attempts to restore the Catholic Stuart family to the throne.

1745: Second rebellion ("the 45") in Scotland led by "Bonnie Prince Charlie" again tries to restore the Stuart monarchy. It is crushed at the Battle of Culloden, 1746.

1793: Wars with France begin; UK threatened with invasion by French forces. France eventually defeated in 1815 at the Battle of Waterloo.

1802: Act of Union brings Ireland into the United Kingdom.

1832: Reform Bills reorganize the way the UK is governed. Further bills follow in 1867, 1884 and 1885.

1870: Education Act makes children's education compulsory and sets up state schools.

1900: British Empire at its most powerful.

1914-18: World War I; Britain fights on the side of the Allies; nearly 660,000 men killed.

1916: Easter Rising in Ireland. Irish Free State set up in 1922; Northern Ireland's six counties remain part of the UK.

1918: Women granted the vote in the UK for the first time.

1939-45: World War II. Britain again fights on the Allied side. UK cities and towns bombed.

1946-51: Many UK industries, such as coal and transportation, nationalized by Labour government.

1947 onward: British colonies and territories granted independence.

1948: National Health Service set up.

1950s onward: Waves of immigration dramatically change makeup of UK society.

1969 onward: Troubles in Northern Ireland.

1979-97: Conservative government privatizes former nationalized industries; extends home and share ownership.

1997: Reforming Labour government elected. Reelected in 2001 and 2005.

1998: Scottish parliament and Welsh assembly set up.

1998: Good Friday Agreement in Northern Ireland.

2005: IRA renounces violence in Northern Ireland.

Glossary and web sites

Angles   Germanic tribesmen who settled in Britain in the fifth century

Catholic   Member of the Christian church who recognizes the Pope as their spiritual leader

Celts   A prehistoric European people, with shared language and culture

Commonwealth   The community of states and dependencies once part of the British Empire

Cymru   The Welsh word for Wales (pronounced "Kumry")

Devolution   The process by which the government in London passes on some of its powers to smaller regional bodies, such as the Scottish parliament

European Union   A grouping of European states that provides economic, commercial, and cultural links, and aims to bring all its members ever closer together

Great Britain   The eighth largest island in the world. It is home to the three separate countries of England, Scotland, and Wales

Greenwich Meridian   Zero degrees longitude – the point from which the world's time zones are calculated

Head of State   A country's main public representative, such as its king, queen, or president

Hereditary monarch   A king or queen who inherits the throne from another member of their family

Hunter-gatherers   People who live entirely by hunting and foraging for food, without any settled agriculture

Highlands   Mountainous region of northern Scotland, known for its great scenic beauty

Loch   A lake or inlet of the sea in Scotland

Luddite   One of a group of early nineteenth-century English workmen who destroyed labor-saving machinery, which had caused them to lose their means of making a living

National Health Service (NHS)   The UK's public health system, paid for by taxes rather than fees charged by doctors

Nonconformist   Protestant religion or worshiper who does not accept the authority of the Church of England

Normans   People from Normandy in northern France, who conquered England in 1066, replacing the Angles and Saxons as rulers

Organic farming   Producing crops and livestock without the use of chemicals and drugs

Papacy   The office of the Pope, leader of the Catholic Church

Paramilitary   A member of one of the armed groups that adopted military-style tactics to wage campaigns of violence in Northern Ireland

Protestant   A follower of one of the Christian groups that split from the Catholic Church in the sixteenth century

Romans   The people of ancient Rome, who built a mighty empire in Europe, and conquered most of Britain in 43 C.E.

Saxons   A warlike people from what is now northwestern Germany, who settled in Britain after the collapse of the Roman Empire

United Kingdom   The state formed by the union of England, Scotland, Wales, and Northern Ireland

---

www.direct.gov.uk Web site of the UK government

www.parliament.uk Official web site of the Houses of Parliament

www.scottish.parliament.uk Official web site of the Scottish parliament

www.wales.gov.uk Welsh assembly web site

www.niassembly.gov.uk Web site of the Northern Ireland assembly

www.london.gov.uk Web site for the Mayor of London and London Assembly

www.statistics.gov.uk Facts and figures from UK census and other official sources

www.bbc.co.uk British Broadcasting Corporation homepage: links to historical and factual information about the UK, news, and radio and television programs

www.visitbritain.com Tourist information and features (multilingual)

Map

COUNTIES OF ENGLAND
(and main administrative centres)

Bedfordshire (Bedford),
Berkshire (Reading),
Buckinghamshire (Aylesbury),
Cambridgeshire (Cambridge),
Cheshire (Chester), Cornwall (Truro),
Cumbria (Carlisle),
Derbyshire (Matlock), Devon (Exeter),
Dorset (Dorchester), Durham (Durham),
East Riding of Yorkshire (Beverley),
East Sussex (Lewes), Essex (Chelmsford),
Gloucestershire (Gloucester),
Greater London, Greater Manchester,
Hampshire (Winchester),
Herefordshire (Hereford),
Hertfordshire (Hertford),
Isle of Wight (Newport),
Kent (Maidstone), Lancashire (Preston),
Leicestershire (Leicester),
Lincolnshire (Lincoln),
Merseyside (Liverpool),
Norfolk (Norwich),
Northamptonshire (Northampton),
Northumberland (Newcastle upon Tyne),
North Yorkshire (Northallerton),
Nottinghamshire (Nottingham),
Oxfordshire (Oxford),
Rutland (Oakham),
Shropshire (Shrewsbury),
Somerset (Taunton),
South Yorkshire (Barnsley),
Staffordshire (Stafford),
Suffolk (Ipswich),
Surrey (Kingston upon Thames),
Tyne and Wear (Newcastle),
Warwickshire (Warwick),
West Midlands (Birmingham),
West Sussex (Chichester),
West Yorkshire (Wakefield),
Wiltshire (Trowbridge),
Worcestershire (Worcester)

SCOTTISH COUNCILS

Aberdeen City, Aberdeenshire, Angus,
Argyll and Bute, Clackmannanshire,
Dumfries and Galloway, Dundee City,
East Ayrshire, East Dunbartonshire,
East Lothian, East Renfrewshire,
Edinburgh City, Eilean Siar, Falkirk, Fife,
Glasgow City, Highland, Inverclyde,
Midlothian, Moray, North Ayrshire,
North Lanarkshire, Orkney Islands,
Perth and Kinross, Renfrewshire,
Scottish Borders, Shetland Islands,
South Ayrshire, South Lanarkshire,
Stirling, West Dunbartonshire,
West Lothian

WELSH COUNCILS

Blaenau Gwent, Bridgend, Caerphilly,
Cardiff, Carmarthenshire, Ceredigion,
Conwy, Denbighshire, Flintshire, Gwynedd,
Isle of Anglesey, Merthyr Tydfil,
Monmouthshire, Neath Port Talbot,
Newport, Pembrokeshire, Powys,
Rhondda Cynon Taff, Swansea, Torfaen,
Vale of Glamorgan, Wrexham

COUNTIES OF NORTHERN IRELAND

Antrim, Armagh, Down, Fermanagh,
Londonderry/Derry, Tyrone

Index